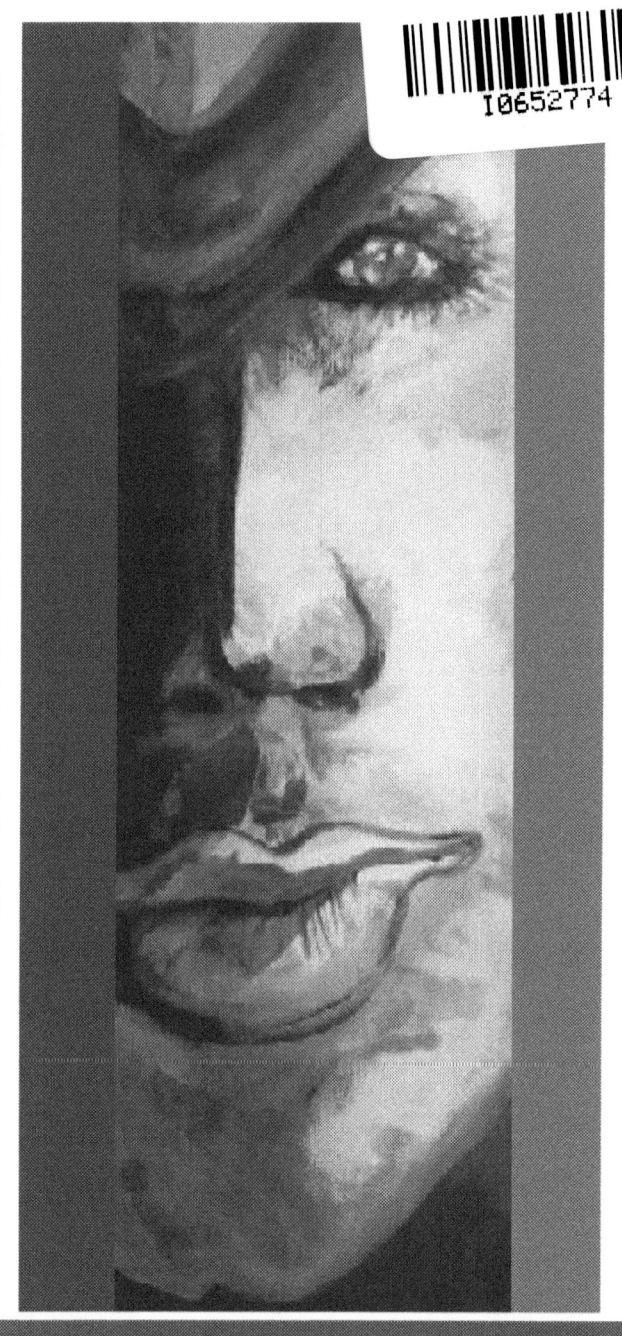

A play by **Molly Brogan** © 1976

Illustrations by Robert Parker

Without
A
Word

By Molly Brogan
Illustrations by Robert Parker

ALSO BY Molly Brogan

- Remember Me
- Chasing Twilight
- Shadow Dancing

D EDICATION

This play is dedicated to Margaret O'Brien, who believed in me every step of the way. Within and without.

Deepest gratitude is also extended to Robert Parker, whose art work graces the cover of this book and runs like blood through the body of this play. Robert is an artist of life who holds the space of highest potential for all of us with every breath he takes.

CHARACTERS

Character #1	Word	character of words, of a million faces, of hot and cold running expression
Character #2	Shadow	of motion, dancer to the next door
Character #3	Dream	a cluster of voices in echo
Character #4	Mirror	the screaming, invisible man
Character #5	Light	colored thought beyond spoken sound

SETTING

The set is comprised of two walls of a room. The wall
most fully facing the audience is of the inside of room.
The room looks sterile. There is a painting on the wall
beside the room's only window. The wall color is grey.
The ceiling is exposed from an extremely short
perspective. Beneath the window is a rocking chair, a
small circular rug beside it. The other wall of the room is
the outside of the room's building, with a door. The door
is made to be slammed, very plain, very subtle lines and
shades of black, white and grey. The roof of the building
can be seen above the door from an extremely short
perspective.

ACT I

Word is sitting in the rocking
chair. Behind the window directly
behind Word, stands Dream.
Shadow lies in fetal position next
to Word's chair. Mirror stands
behind the door, unseen. As the
lights come up, Dream is
mumbling, Word is humming,
Mirror is yelling softly and shadow
is till. As Word begins his
monologue, all other activity
stops.

Word

Sitting here, just sitting here, damn it. Not even sitting
here now, just sitting here. Probably've been sitting here
longer than any statistic could prove. Never could
understand those proofs anyway. Just wouldn't connect.
As if my mind had a mind of its own. As if, when I
touched on possibility, when I felt as if the possible were
mine, my mind would take it and pound it trough my
body, and my body would take it in action to the man
next door. And together we would dream of showing it
to the world, write it down, put it in color. And everyone
would stand erect to watch it. I could almost see their
little minds taking it in, giving it to their bodies. And on
those cold, damp nights...

Light

I'd dream of vibrating pillars, merging into a gigantic white sphere that melted into darkness.

Word

And I'd awaken to the dark, and know that the darkness, both inside and out was all that I knew. And I'd silently wait for morning. Funny though, I haven't seen that man for a long, long time.

Dream

Dream together into darkness, know the white, melted, taking giving, inside little bodies, out of minds

See their bodies giving into the darkness. Wait for the merging of little minds. Awaken to the cold, damp dream of melting morning, inside pillars, white spheres out.

Shadow

During dream, shadow stands, shuffles over to the door, reaches the door and knocks loudly. The door opens very slowly and slightly and then slams. Shadow caresses the door once with his/her hands and then shuffles back to his/her position next to word. During this, dream is saying:

Dream

Darkness behind darkness behind darkness behind darkness behind…

Word

I'm bursting inside, can you hear me? My thoughts are screaming...

Light

It seems that whenever I reach out, when I think that I seen another person here with me, sitting below my window, I'm only reaching into the dark.

Word

And I'm alone, sitting, looking out of my window at the thousands of indifferent faces glued to their rigid little bodies, and the only mergence I can see is in my minds eye, the only color in the dead of night.

Light

And in my dream all those faces are of me. All those faces mirror my solitary action, yet most do not resemble me or my action. As if they were created through another man's eye, another's hazed feelings of me, all fantastic feelings of course. And I ask myself, how can I possibly touch those feelings, those fleeting images as they stand above time, above space?

Word

How to make my creation theirs, and theirs mine? And
how to link all of this to the continuous stream of
thought, set in manner of opposites for talk, for screams
and whispers and long dull moans?

Dream

Opposites scream for talk in fantastic images of another
feeling, creation of how stands in time through space for
dream. through my eye I see myself in feelings and
screams of images, streams of whispers, fleeting thought
another continuous mirror

Shadow

*During dream shadow stands, shuffles swiftly across the stage,
knocks on the door.*

Mirror

*The door opens widely, mirror appears wearing a mask of word, is
seen only briefly and the door slams.*

Shadow

*Shadow shakes his/her head and returns to the rug in the same
manner in which he/she left it while dream:*

Dream

<u>Must</u> <u>know,</u> <u>must</u> <u>know</u> <u>how.</u> <u>Must</u> <u>know,</u> <u>must</u> <u>know</u>
<u>how.</u> <u>Must</u> <u>know,</u> <u>must</u> <u>know</u> <u>how</u>

Word

That man invades me through his evasion. When I was a
child, lying in bed, falling into dream…

Light

I'd see his dark, flowing figure traveling a billowing path
that is covered by tall, unmoving trees on either side.
And the man moves slowly, easily towards a light that
radiates at the end of his direction (or is it the beginning?)
And as I try to follow secretly, unseen, the path becomes
fluid, and I cannot take a step. My feet become immersed
and the path sucks me in like quicksand. And I strain and
fight to gain every inch as the path rises and falls, rises
and falls. I can only see him when the path has fallen.
But as he walks it, it remains smooth, as if he were merely
floating above it.

Word

And now that path drives me crazy, drives me in the light
as well as the dark. For at times, as I sit beneath my
window, and think of paying the man a visit, I see the
path rising up and enveloping my inner vision, turning the
light and color into darkness. And so I never go to the
door. Instead, I sit, frantically wanting to take old of
another hand…

Light

Of a million hands at once, and to have all those hands merge into one gentle touch, a touch that is blind to the ends of a string. That stands as the basis of the fusion. And through the fusion…

Word

We can turn our inner color into forms for the hand to hold, to squeeze and mold and contain.

Light

But who in their right chair could ever think such things?

Word

Who could ever hope to shatter such an invisible separation? For when I turn and look, what I see rushes through my body at such speeds that I can never hope to catch it. And all the different looks…

Light

And all the different bodies…

Word

And all the different speeds. I'd love to break this damn window. Maybe there's a tool next door. Something to hold and swing and…But how can I return there, when in my dream…

Shadow

Shadow stands, shuffles in quick circles to the door and knocks very softly.

Mirror

The door opens, mirror is without a face. They stand for a moment looking at each other, mirror yells and slams the door.

Shadow

Shadow shuffles slowly backwards to the rug.

Word

Perhaps now you see why I sit in my chair.

Light

Never moving from this space that gained its limit long ago.

Word

It is here that the line was drawn in time, a line that marked the cessation of growth. And one day I looked into the window and saw that may face had changed…and I remembered that the look in my eye, as I looked at myself in my youth had been wide, direct. Now I can't catch the eye of my reflection, for the grays and the chair have pulled me upward, away from it. My reflection now seems to be looking outward, towards the trees and the faces just as I do, and it will not meet me. It sometimes seems as if my thoughts and all their connectedness belong outside of this window…

Light

Among the trees and the synthetic light.

Word

As if my senses and feelings rode behind those thoughts, making their feeble attempt to catch them, evading me in their invasion, leaving me empty and alone in the darkness of night. So, in order for my mind to survive, it begins to dream, dragging my body through restless slumber. And it is there and then that my passions are turned to emotive color.

Light

And it is here that my mind oversteps the boundaries of time and space. And here, I fly over the barren, white, luminescent mound, circling it. And as I descend slowly in my spiral, I begin to swing my hand downward, towards the white, flinging my shadow of invisibility towards it. And as it strikes the mound erupts in volcanic color and the color breeds flowing form. And my circles get wider and wider and I fall lower and lower until I become completely immersed in the color, falling aster and faster through it…

Word

And in this speed I take my comfort.

Light

And in this color my mind takes life.

Word

And when I awake my imagination is free to wander through possibilities unheard, but seen.

Light

Untouched but felt.

Word

But how can I place this vision outside the window, fling it through the faces whose eyes are open, whose eyes see me through their own light, and not through their image of mine?

Dream

Take comfort in circles of color that fall and wander through vision outside, completely unheard, but felt, open, seen through image

Fling faces trough eyes of possibilities and color takes
live, circles become speed, vision becomes fantasy, free to
open form

Awake to wander untouched, seen outside through faces,
through me in color, in mind, getting wider and faster in
comfort, possibility felt outside vision through image

Shadow

*Shadow stands slowly while word is ending and moves
simultaneously with dream's echo, shuffling over to the door in
spastic motions, fast then slow, and scrapes his/her nails over the
door while whimpering.*

Mirror

*The door opens, mirror can be seen wearing a blank white face. The
door slams shut.*

Shadow

Shadow crawls back to the rug, still puling.

Word

Each...one of us, apart and alone from the us of
each...one, two of us...one for two that's what I say, but
when, at the very first blink of a restless night, I see a
light coming from the center of our separation, from the
wall that stands closest to my head, that stands to contain
dream, I think of him... in terms of two for one.

Shadow and Word

Both Shadow and Word stand and approach the door in identical action, moving very close to one another. The steps are short, laborious. During this, word is saying:

Word

And as I walk in time, over the clear path towards the door, my mind asks, two for one? The idea could never have color, how? They're simply numbers, lines and forms in constant process, simultaneous division/multiplication, like all harmonies…but it is vision that colors meaning, as it reaches outward.

Shadow and Word

As Word speaks the word "outward," both shadow and word have reached the door and slam their fist on it. The door opens.

Word

You have no color, the mask of your harmony invisible. And so – I beg your pardon, Who…

Shadow and Word

On the word "who" the door slams, Shadow and Word return to their positions, shuffling, raising their arms so that they are perpendicular to their body and then dropping them, in opposing motions, while Dream:

Dream

<u>Walk</u> <u>towards</u> <u>time</u> <u>like</u> <u>vision</u> <u>that</u> <u>colors</u> <u>harmonies</u> <u>of</u>
<u>numbers,</u> <u>forms</u> <u>of</u> <u>process,</u> <u>lines</u> <u>of</u> <u>idea</u>

<u>Process</u> <u>asks</u> <u>the</u> <u>idea</u> <u>how</u> <u>it</u> <u>is</u> <u>beaten,</u> <u>when</u> <u>time</u> <u>is</u> <u>the</u>
<u>path</u> <u>of</u> <u>color</u> <u>and</u> <u>forms</u> <u>in</u> <u>the</u> <u>reaches</u> <u>of</u> <u>numbers</u>

Word

If only I could create something, just one thing. Just
once, I'd like to mold some thing into a shape that I
could hand in offering, through the window. Some thing
that the young, and the old, redundant faces could put
into their space, and so see and envision for themselves.

Light

Some thing I could fling through their invisible eyelids to
etch itself upon their fragmented thoughts, connecting
them. So that they could sit back, and envision the shape
that they color.

Word

...some – thing that would lure them into their sacred,
private playground. That would draw them into dream
and restful, plaintive nights.

Light

Some thing apart from them, that they suck in through
their senses like milk from a white, swelling source. And

the fluid rushes through their veins and enlivens every inch of them until they moan softly Until they are fully redeemed.

Word

Some thing to give them all a part of myself, so that I can see them facing me squarely, in my mind. And as this thing ascends from the very depths of my darkness, I can't stand it. I feel that I must reach to touch. Reach so that my darkness comes more easily into the light.

Light

And so, I am.

Shadow

Shadow stands and moves sideways to the door. Reaches it and flings his/her body against it, then slowly moves away from it.

Mirror

The door opens slowly and mirror appears, unmasked, and yells.

Shadow

Shadow falls to the floor and begins to squirm back to the rug while the door is slamming.

Word

Damn, I hate this place. Sitting here day after day,
counting the time by number. And it seems my frantic
mind will only play melodic discord. Almost as if the
backwards-forwards-inbetweenness had no connection,
had no unity with where I sit, just sit...

Dream

Sit sit sit sit sit sit sit sit sit sit sit sit sit sit sit sit sit sit sit
sit sit sit sit sit sit...

Word

Look at this, my eyes are constantly bombarded with gray
and dark and how am I to breathe? To feel all that is
around me, to feel without touch? If only I could find
some light, the colors may change. Oh, what that light
would do for my wandering fantasy: the reds, the blues,
the greens, like those that waver beyond the window. I
close my eyes...

Light

That dream...where I stood enveloped in darkness, mist
rolling at my feet. And as I bent to touch that mist, it
rose and turned to light. And with the light I could see
the colors, and the forms, saturated with the color. And
all of those shapeless forms turned to smiling faces,
whose eyes told me then, that they knew of my discovery.
And in that dream the faces turned to white, and my
thoughts, the ones the eyes had conveyed, blended with
the light, with the white. And the faces no longer needed
eyes, because they knew without seeing. It seemed as

though we created that light, and in that creation we became the window.

Word

But dreams end. And here is my window. If only I could get inside this window. It would seem as though, if I could meet my own eye…and return to the window…or, the door…

Dream

I created the seeing through faces that needed the inside of my light that could no longer meet the dreams, I return to my own

Faces no longer needed to get inside the light, the creation knew that the eyes became an end without seeing

Here my eye is light that created my window as though inside were a door that needed eyes because in that creation the end became the dream

My own door is here inside my window no longer needing eyes as though dream created eyes and knew the longer need, the light, the window

Shadow

During Dream, Shadow stands, shuffles toward the door quickly and taps gently.

Mirror

The door opens fully and then slams shut, mirror unseen.

Shadow

Shadow returns to the rug slowly, waving arms in circular motion until she/he reaches the rug, then drops down.

Word

Perhaps if I never slept, never dreamt...

Light

At least I could escape those visions of infants rolling faster and faster over desolate, white hills, faster, faster, until my mind screams for release.

Word

If I could just sit, and think of the inclusive sunsets I saw in my youth, of the oceans where I sat to watch and think for time spent. Of the cliffs I could climb to envision the towering cities. And those cities that I would explore and search for a glimpse of my own image.

Light

I can see myself, finding that image and savoring every line, every color that appeared visible, that lent itself to my own visions. Then I can take that color, and return it to the image of the city, and the city would bloom, its night would break into dew laden morning.

Word

And I would take that sheath of exposed invisibility and
offer it in word, and every eye came to know the word.
But now it seems as if I am forced to carefully measure
my word, turn it into possibility…and then drag it
through the long thin string that covers my window,
inhibits the light. And now these thoughts come only in
sitting. I cannot even take them next door. Perhaps…if I
turned the vision to word…

Dream

The color knew and would break the night to return to
the image and its word and its city, then the string of
possibility measured word

Its night would break the vision into morning, the long
dream, offer thoughts in exposed word to carefully turn
through invisibility taking them to the city of even light,
every window

Offer the word to sheath the image but turn the string in
long measured sitting as it returns and takes the color of
itself, forced through the window of my if I

Shadow

*During dream, Shadow stands, covers mouth with both hands, and
shuffles toward the door, flinging his body from side to side.
Reaching the door he knocks on it with his head, hands still over
mouth.*

Mirror

The door opens, and Mirror appears with a mask, one half black the other white. Mirror steps back into the darkness of the doorway and slams the door.

Shadow

Shadow limps back to the rug, one hand over mouth, the other over eyes.

Word

Oh, that dream, dream again…

Dream

Dream again, dream again, dream again, dream again, dream again…

Word

(addressing the audience) Close your eyes. Yes, close your eyes damn it! Can't you see, look, can't you see?

Light

The solid black, fragmented lines falling through white, falling in straight paths, falling into children's open mouths, in harmonic succession. And as the children swallow sections of line, they burst into color, each child a different color.

Word

Can't you see it in your mind, in your imagination? You're here AND now, not like me, not like me. You only see me here, but I can see you here and now, here and now…as if my vision were not my word, not my word…

Dream

Dream dream dream dream dream dream dream dream dream dream dream…

Word

Damn him, he's taken my words.

Dream

My words my words my words my words my words my words my words…

Word

I cannot even see myself now. If I could but take the harmonies of sound, of line inside my head and place them outside, give them as offering, to an image, to a thought, to all thoughts that need to become…

Light

The would be a joining of hands. There the invisible would be seen. There my image would pass into theirs.

Word

Then they too would see it, put it into sound and word, write it down, speak it, sing it, hold it, cuddle it. Then my words would scatter, into all their different spaces, and each would be carried through the mind in past, in present, in future.

Shadow

Shadow stands, shuffles to the door while dream:

Dream

Image pass to their hold trough my words carried in spaces through future words sing to hold down present, scatter to cuddle future, see to speak of past

Write it to speak it, cuddle it to sing it, scatter it to hold it, image of mind in space

Mirror

Door opens and shuts immediately.

Shadow

Shadow fall to knees and shuffles back to the rug as dream:

Dream

<u>Words</u> <u>words</u> <u>words</u> <u>words</u> <u>words</u> <u>words</u> <u>words</u> <u>words</u>
<u>words</u> <u>words</u> <u>words</u>…

Word

If only I could get into their minds, get to their words,
since I cannot leave this chair to accept their offering. If
only I could understand, could know exactly how they
color me, color themselves, then maybe…

Light

If only I could crawl behind their eyes and see what it is
they select for their minds, select for the feelings that flow
from their senses beneath their soft white skins. The
feelings that build and subside like ocean waves.
Together we could ride those waves. And in this
togetherness we could create a life for the ocean, a level
for its motion.

Word

We would ride those waves as I do now, alone, in
dream…Imagine – floating on top of the surf that rises,
in rhythmic, undulating changes. Rises to meet the white
sky. And as it descends, the sky is cast with the color of a
prismic sunset. But now, in this space, my thoughts sink
through coherent light, falling lower and lower into my

darkness, searching for a semblance of time. And as it sinks, my mind tells me that there is no connection. That my thoughts cannot be theirs, even in word, in knowing, in screaming…for my scream is silent.

Dream

Space sinks in mink like a semblance of screaming connection, like a silent thought that falls to meet a final word, the word that sinks in sunset

Their my sinks in thought like darkness, searching the silent light for connection, for semblance like a scream searching for space

My mind sinks, searching for connection, searching for the light of thought in space, lowering the scream into a final, knowing heart

The connection sinks in word, a final, even darkness as in my heart a sunset screams for light, searching for a silent knowing

Shadow

During dream, shadow moves across the stage using her/his arms, in almost a swimming motion, reaches the door, and claws it with his/her hands like a dog paddling.

Mirror

The door opens, mirror appears with a mask painted with the colors of a sunset. Mirror rocks head back and forth a few times, then slams the door.

Shadow

Shadow rolls back to the rug.

Word

Oh, that door...

Dream

That door that door that door that door that door that door that door that door

Word

Thoughts and visions

Dream

Thoughts and visions thoughts and visions thoughts and visions thoughts and visions

Light

Thoughts come in vision.

Word

That's it! What is known is know through vision. I take it from me, and give it to their words, so that they may have it. But how do they take it?

Dream

Take it take it take it take it take it take it take it take it take it take it take it take it

Word

Take this silent offering that screams in word. How can this window be? When what I see within, they see without. Without me, but with me.

Shadow

Shadow stands and begins to shuffle in circles.

Dream

Within without within without within without within without within without

Word

I am within, I am without. Here in this space, now looking to see the vision welling up inside in waves…

Light

I see it, I feel it, I understand it, I know it, I take it, I give it, they see it, they feel it, they take it, they give it...

Word

Yes, I dreamt it last night.

Light

I dreamt myself sitting above a massive white sphere, with color revolving, the color mine, evolving around it.

Word

And in the dream I reached for the color and as I reached and touched, the color entered me, entered my body and rushed through my veins like a surging stream. And as the color took shape in my mind, the shape of a million faces, color poured out of my eyes and returned to its orbit around the sphere.

Shadow

Shadow approaches the door in circular steps as dream:

Dream

I you he she it we you they I you he she it we you they I you he she it we you they

---

Mirror

The door opens, Mirror appears wearing a white, circular mask painted with orbital colors. Shadow and Mirror meet in motion.

Dream

<u>Me</u> you <u>him</u> her <u>it</u> us <u>you</u> them <u>me</u> you <u>him</u> her <u>it</u> us <u>you</u> them <u>me</u> you <u>him</u> her <u>it</u> us <u>you</u> them

Mirror

Mirror recedes, the door slams.

Shadow

Shadow returns to rug in circular steps and stands while dream:

Dream

<u>I</u> me <u>you</u> you <u>he</u> him <u>she</u> her <u>it</u> it <u>we</u> us <u>you</u> you <u>they</u> them <u>I</u> me <u>you</u> you <u>he</u> him <u>she</u> her <u>it</u> it <u>we</u> us <u>you</u> you <u>they</u> them

Word

But what if...loathsome chair, I am not a child again.

Dream

Am am not am am not am am not am am not am am not
am am not am am not

Word

But what if…

Shadow

Shadow begins to move in semi circles near the rug.

Dream

Him she her it you they   you I he you us them   you you
I them him it   me he she I you them   I you him she us
me   I me him them us you

Shadow

Shadow freezes but remains standing

Word

That's it, all lines, all lines, but each one of two a different
line. But all lines! And so I give my line in offering, and
all those faces take my line, and rearrange it, but the
line…

Shadow

Shadow begins moving in semi circles again

Dream

The line the line the line the line the line the line the line
the line the line the line

Shadow

Shadow freezes and remains standing.

Word

I must be this window. I am the window. And through
this window I become all faces, and within this window
all numbers and words and visions become aligned. My
mind can see. My dream looks to find the light of the
sunset, the beginning and the end of surging, rolling
pathways. And in that dream my body pulsates with
silent scream, within and without. And in this room now,
my imagination awakens. My mind screams to me.

Dream

See the number's visions of the setting sun through the I
am of this window, the dream I fly to find with silent
speed

My screams find light in the room within the light of the
sunset, and at this beginning, at this end, my colors dream
within and without a path aligned setting

My dream flys to find the rolling sunset, surging in the
end of a silen beginning, as words become colors that my
mind screams to find

Light looks to the beginning for the silent end so that
dream can see

The numbers of all faces aligned with vision, and this
screams to me

Shadow

During dream, shadow races to the door, taps fingers lightly upon it.

Mirror

*Door opens. Mirror appears covered in colored veils and begins to
shed them. As the door closes, one veil becomes caught in it.*

Shadow

Shadow fingers the veil and runs back to the rug.

Word

Scream.

Dream

Scream scream scream scream scream scream scream
scream scream scream scream

Word

Perhaps there is no scream, oh no, oh no, all this talk of scream...and now I see that my only real scream is the light that I ride when I become that man in my dream...

Light

The one that rides the path above its motion, that takes the line and changes it from color to white and white to color, and so, into a million faces, all swallowing the line and bursting into color...

Word

And this is no longer a dream. It is here, while the room is full, and there, when the room is empty. Then, when the room is not...am, am not, is, is not...

Dream

Is not am not is not am not is not am not is not am not is not am not

Word

Take it in and fling it through your bodies with me. See it, feel it...

Dream

See it feel it see it feel it see it feel it see it feel it see it feel it see it feel it see it feel it

Word

Funny though, long long time…

Dream

Funny though long long time   funny though long long time   funny though long long time

Shadow

Shadow falls to the floor and lands on her/his back, and pushes across the stage with his/her feet. He/she reaches the door and slams on it with his/her feet.

Mirror

The door opens and mirror is without a mask, face unseen. Mirror yells and closes the door.

Shadow

Shadow curls into fetal position and slithers back to the rug.

Word

And if it were possible to know, I would stand erect to watch it.

Shadow

Shadow stands.

Word

Stand as motionless as an ageless tree, stand to become the illuminated sphere that erupts in volcanic color…as if…what if…

Dream

As if what if as if what if as if what if as if what if as if what if as if what if as if what if

Shadow and Word

Walk together as one to the door, open the door and pick up the masks and veils left by Mirror throughout and throughin. They walk over to the chair and them, one by one, through the window, to Light. They turn, pull down a roll of cellophane which is in back of the setting, out of view, and wrap themselves in it.

Meet Shadow and Word on center stage. As they all meet and are fused, colored balloons pour out of the window and a white sheet falls on them from above. All fall onto the floor and move slowly beneath it, colored lights flashing on them. The sound of popping balloons can be heard in the background. Fade out...

End